Imp

Marjorie Darke

Illustrated by
MARGARET
CHAMBERLAIN

William Heinemann Ltd
A division of Reed Consumer Books Ltd
Michelin House
81 Fulham Road
London SW3 6RB

LONDON . MELBOURNE . AUCKLAND

First published 1985
Reprinted twice, reprinted 1992, 1994
Text © 1985 Marjorie Darke
Illustrations © 1985 Margaret Chamberlain
ISBN 0 434 93028 8

Printed in Italy by Olivotto

A school pack of BANANA BOOKS 7-12 is
available from Heinemann Educational Books
ISBN 0 435 00101 9

HAVE YOU EVER had something really weird happen to you? Something that makes your brains feel as if they've been put in a mixer and whisked round till they're all in a fizz?

Well, it was like that with me and my pocket calculator.

I'd been itching to have one for ages. Not any old calculator. I'd picked out a special one in Carey's window, down the High Street. It was shiny white and had IMP M–1 printed above its little screen. Underneath were coloured buttons – grey, blue, yellow. Soon as I

1

saw it I made up my mind to buy it. Took a lot of saving up though. Weeks of pocket money. And I did odd jobs for people. By the end of October I only needed 50p and Mum said she'd give it me if I helped clean our car. Les wanted to help as well. Les is my brother and he's saving for a Space Invaders game.

While we washed and polished on Saturday morning, Les kept on trying to scare me, telling about all these spooky things. He thinks he's dead clever at this, but he isn't.

'Did you know our car's haunted?'

I didn't answer.

'Honest! A headless motorcyclist sits next to your place in the back seat.'

I still didn't answer.

'Some people do see ghosts easier than others,' he went on. 'I'd just got out of the bath last night when this

seethrough slime from the gravel pits
crawled out of the plughole.'

'How d'you know it came from the
gravel pits?' I asked.

'I saw through my window.'

'But you were having a bath!'

'Not all the time. I looked through
the window before I got in the bath and
saw it slithering over the building site
. . . it dripped all over our bathroom
floor.'

'Oh, Les!' Mum said, and gave us our 50ps.

I didn't hang about. Les's stories don't scare me. But I *was* scared somebody might have got to Carey's first and bought my calculator.

They hadn't. There it was on the shelf.

'Two from the left,' I told the man behind the counter.

He took it down. 'For school is it?'

I said: 'No.' Then: 'Well p'raps,' because I wanted to take it to show my mates, specially Elise. She's my best mate and she's always coming to school with new things. Last Monday she had a tortoise ring, and Friday before, a pencil-case shaped like a banana.

'I see!' he said, winking just as if he knew what was in my mind. Not a quick wink, sort of slow motion so each

eye looked as if it belonged in a different face. It wasn't half weird. But that's not the really weird thing I'm going to tell you.

Back home I took the calculator out
of its box and put it on the kitchen
table. It looked wonderful. I didn't
want to try it out yet. I just wanted to
look at it and think about it being mine.

But then Les came in on his way to
get a Coke from the fridge. 'Let's see!'
He zoomed over and picked up my
calculator before I could stop him.
'I.M.P. . . . what sort of cheap tat's
that? You should've got an I.B.M.
They're the best.'

'No, I shouldn't!' He thinks he
knows everything about calculators and
computers and things. I took it off him
before he could start messing about,
and switched on. Then I added up our
family ages. Les 12, Mum 32, Dad 34,
me 9. I divided the answer by 29,
because today was the 29th of October.

The calculator showed 3. I liked that.
Oggie's birthday is today and he's
three. Oggie is our cat. He's white with
one green eye and one blue.

'Tell you what,' Les said. 'I'll give you some numbers to work out while I do them in my head. See who wins.'

I knew he'd work out the answer before we even started. He's dead clever at numbers. But I said 'Okay' all the same.

'43 times 30 add 92 take away 1381 . . .'

'505.505,' I shouted before he could get in first.

'No, it isn't. The answer's 1. You must've pressed the wrong buttons.'

'I didn't.'

'Must've. Try again.'

I tried.

'317716.14.' I held it out, turning it round for Les to see.

Upside down the numbers looked like letters. 'hI.gILLIE' it said clear as clear. Gillie – that's me! In small and big

letters. It wasn't half a surprise.

'Duff!' Les said firmly, and taking
my calculator from me, pressed some
other buttons. I was still looking at it
upside down and saw my name
disappear and the screen write:
'SOS.SOS'.

To find out what that was in numbers I practically had to stand on my head!

'505.505'. *The same answer as before.*

'Duff as duff,' Les said. 'Should say 123.' He prodded a few more buttons.

'hELLO.LES' wrote the calculator.

Of course Les didn't know. He wasn't looking at the screen upside down like me. He just went on trying different buttons and the words kept changing.

'SOS.SOS' 'SOS.gILL' 'LOOSE.I' 'SOS.LES' 'LOOSE.I'

A little tickle like flies' feet began walking down the back of my neck.

It was as if someone was talking to us through my calculator. But who? I wasn't going to breathe a word to Les. If I did he'd want to get a screwdriver and open up my calculator to see the works and find out what was going on, and there wouldn't be a hope of stopping him.

Just then the doorbell rang. I took the calculator with me to keep it safe when I went to see who was there.

'Hello!' Elise said. She was wearing new jeans and had her yellow hair frizzed out round her head. She had a new Friends of the Earth badge as well, pinned to her red sweat shirt. 'I came to see what you were doing.'

I showed her my pocket calculator.

She only gave it a quick look. Anybody would have thought it was dead ordinary. A pack of felt tips or something. 'Sums?' she said, as if I was daft.

'It *talks*,' I told her and then wished I hadn't.

'Calculators don't talk.'

I couldn't back out. 'Mine does.' We were going into the kitchen now and Les heard.

'Does what?'

'Gillie says her calculator talks.'

'Well it *writes*,' I said.

Les just had to see for himself, *of course*. He took the calculator off me. Then Elise took it off him. They kept pressing buttons like mad. Saying things like 'Ooo' and 'Blimey' and 'Hey look at that' and I couldn't get to see *anything*.

Then Elise started to giggle. 'Look
. . . "goloshes" . . . that's what my
Grandad wears over his shoes to keep
out the wet. *Goloshes*!' and she fell
about laughing and trod on Oggie who
was asleep by the chair leg. He let out a
yowl and fled through the backdoor
which was open a crack. I shoved
between them and got to see
'gO.OggIE' on the upside down screen.
Then 'Oh.hEEhEE' just as if the
calculator was giggling too. I'm sure I
hadn't touched any buttons.

The others had seen as well.

'What we *ought* to do . . .' Les began.

I held my breath.

'. . . is make a list of all the words it's written. We might get a clue then. Find out what's gone wrong.'

Phew! That was a near thing. I'd been so sure that he meant to use the screwdriver on my calculator. Open it up – break it probably. But lists were okay. Les makes hundreds of lists. He

has lots of notebooks with things in them like the names of all the West Ham soccer players that have ever lived. And train numbers. And years and years of cricket Test Match scores.

'Put down "Hi Elise",' Elise said. 'I saw it write that, and "SOS" about fifty million times.'

'Six,' Les told her. 'Don't exaggerate.'

He likes using long words. He can really get up your nose when he's getting niggly about the right numbers of everything. I could see he'd got up Elise's nose.

'Well . . . however many, it still means Save Our Souls. That's a way of calling for help if you're shipwrecked and are drowning.' She had stopped laughing.

'How d'you know?' Les asked.

'My Dad told me.'

Elise's Dad is a sailor, so I believed her.

Les fished a notebook out of his jeans back pocket and started to write: 'Hi Elise, SOS, Loose I, Go Hole, Soggie, Goloshes . . .' He always talks aloud when he's writing down.

Elise said: 'The first bit makes sense – SOS and all that – but why "go hole" and "soggy" and "goloshes"? I mean, it's a load of rubbish.'

'Perhaps it's telling us to wear our wellies because the hole is soggy. Only it can't write wellies so it puts goloshes instead,' I suggested.

'What hole?' Elise asked.

I didn't know, and Les said, 'I don't think they can *really* be calls for help. Maybe the factory put in the wrong sort of transistor circuit. Made it into a

radio receiver instead of a calculator.
We ought to phone 999. Tell the
police.'

'What would we say?' I asked.

'Somebody's drowning, silly.'

'The sea is miles away,' Elise said.

'What difference does that make?
Radio waves can go right out to Mars
and back, easy. Anyway there's plenty
of other water round here for boats.
The canal, and the river down past the
church . . .'

'And the gravel pits,' I put in to help keep his mind off screwdrivers.

'Yes. Plenty of places to drown.'

Elise said: 'Just SOS is no good. They have to say where they are. If we told the police it's Gillie's calculator that keeps getting these messages, they'd think we were off our heads.'

It did sound daft.

'P'raps we should take a look inside,' Les said at last.

'Don't you dare!' I snatched my calculator away from him.

Dad came in just then to start making dinner. It was his turn today. Just as well or Les and I might have had a fight. Elise said she ought to go for her dinner. Her Mum said not to be late.

'I'll come back after though, if that's okay?'

'Stay for tea,' Dad invited.

'Can she stay the night?' I asked quick, while he was in an inviting mood. I'd always wanted Elise to stay, so we could talk in bed in the dark.

'If her Mum says she can.'

Elise went, and Les and I had to help Dad, but I didn't mind one bit. Dad said my calculator was A1. *And* we had egg and chips, my favourite. I broke the eggs in a cup for Dad. I'm good at that. While we were eating I was dead scared in case Les started telling how my calculator talked. Mum would be sure to say: 'Take it back to the shop.' I didn't want to change it. Anyway, he didn't. Afterwards though, he kept following me about asking and asking to open it up. He even fetched the set of pocket screwdrivers he had for his last birthday.

'Go on. I won't spoil it. Promise I'll put it together again.'

'Yes, go on, let him, Gillie,' Elise begged. She had been home and come back again.

I could see there was going to be trouble. She was just as curious as Les. I was feeling a little bit curious myself. Also I'd always wanted to have a go with Les's screwdrivers. 'Oh, all right,' I said. 'But only if you let me undo the screws.' I think he was going to say no, but Elise said: 'Go on, Les. It's only fair.'

So I got to use the screwdrivers after all. I took out the two batteries first, then undid the screws. That part was dead easy. But the top of the case didn't want to lift off. I had to help it with the screwdriver and Les shouted at me and that made my hand slip.

CRACK!

21

I nearly fell off the bed, the noise was so sudden. Just like a firework going off. At the same time an electric shock buzzed through my fingers and up my arm as the top flipped back. There was a flash too. A spark shot from inside my calculator and went darting round the room. We only saw because it was glowing so brightly – it was travelling that fast.

Of course I dropped the calculator. Luckily we were all sitting on my bed at the time so it didn't have far to fall. Elise bunched up, hugging her knees as if she was trying to keep her feet safe from an escaped mouse.

The spark suddenly burst into a small flame.

'Fire!' Elise yelled.

This time we did fall off the bed and made a dash for the door. I was last. The others never stopped, but I did because from behind us came this

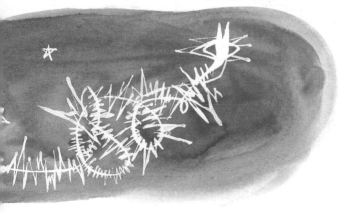

sudden high squeaky noise. Flea laughter. That's what it sounded like. Bouncing off the walls. I looked round. The flame was still shooting about. *But there was no smoke nor smell of burning.*

The flea laughter switched off and the flame seemed to grow elbows. Like when someone puts their hands on their hips. I'm sure I saw a face in it too, with pointed ears. The flame kept on whizzing about, so it was hard to get a proper look. Then I heard a tinny voice talking very fast. As if it was a tape played at the wrong speed. A lot of the words ran together but I did catch: 'Free free,' and then some more flea laughs.

The flame darted at the window and bounced back. 'Loose I . . . Gillie . . . go hole . . . soggy . . .'

I'm sure that's what it said. Those strange words about some soggy hole. What could they mean?

The others had gone tearing downstairs, and the next thing I knew Mum and Dad came tearing up to put out the fire. Les and Elise were close behind. I don't know if it was extra draught as Dad pushed the door wide open, but the flame puffed out. The voice shut up too.

'Where's the fire? What's going on? Is this your idea of a joke?' He sounded a bit shirty. Then he caught sight of my wrecked calculator and he *was* shirty. 'How did this happen?'

'It was all Gillie's fault . . .'

'Les made me . . .' we said together.

Dad's eyebrows came together in a line like they do when he's cross. 'Frightening the life out of us. *Fire*!' The way he said 'fire' showed he thought us a right pair of fried eggs.

But there *was* a smell of burning now.

'Oh . . . the toast!' Mum gasped and went galloping back down again.

We had tea after that. Mum had to make fresh toast, and there were jam doughnuts as well. Great! Except jam from mine squirted out all over the tablecloth when I bit into it. As I went to fetch a cloth to wipe it up, the lights went out. Which made Mum and me bump into each other in the doorway. She was fetching candles.

'Power cut!' *She* sounded cross now. 'Typical. That means cold supper on a cold night.'

'We've got the gas fire to keep us warm,' Dad said.

'Huh!' She sounded as if she didn't believe him. 'Listen to that wind. I called and called that stupid cat, Oggie,

before tea but he won't come in.
Raining cats and dogs out there it is.'

'He'll have company then,' Dad said.

That was so funny I forgot about my
calculator long enough to laugh.
Nobody else thought it was funny.

'No telly,' Les said gloomily. But he
cheered up when Dad suggested telling
ghost stories by candlelight.

'Darren saw a spectre when he was
clearing up his fishing rods down by the
gravel pits,' Les said. Darren is Les's
mate. He's allowed to go to the gravel
pits on his own. We can't. Mum says
it's too dangerous. We might get stuck

in the boggy part. Or fall in and drown.

'At least,' Les went on, 'he didn't see all of it. Just these great eyes like lamps . . .'

'Car headlights?' Dad suggested.

'Headlights don't slice rabbits in two. Laser-beam eyes, that's what they were. This rabbit went belting across the patch of grass in front of the marshy part . . . and you know that heap of earth? Well, these eyes showed over the top of that. The rabbit got in the way and bingo! You should've seen it – head and front legs still running while . . .'

'What's a spectre?' I interrupted quickly. I didn't want to hear any more. When Les gets stuck into telling about gory things, it's horrible.

'A spectre is a ghost that inspects other ghosts. Like bus inspectors check buses to make sure they're running to time.'

'Oh, Les!' Mum said. She's always saying that.

'It's true. Honest!'

We ran out of ghost stories after a bit and played snakes and ladders instead. Elise got really excited and kept on winning. When it was time for bed the lights still hadn't come back on. So we took a candle to light the way. The candleflame flickered and made weird moving shapes on the staircase wall and ceiling. Skinny pointing fingers and birds' legs hopping up and down. They

didn't look like our stairs at all. Of course I knew it was only shadows made from the bannisters and us climbing. But it *was* weird.

Earlier I'd told Elise about lying in bed and talking in the dark.

'Oo, lovely,' she'd said in a flat voice.

After we'd undressed and cleaned our teeth I found out why she wasn't too keen. She's an Olympic gold medal winner at sleeping! She got into my bed (I was sleeping on the camp bed), pulled the duvet over her head and went out like a light.

I did try waking her, but all she did was snore. She sounded like a drummer in a shed.

I stayed wide awake. For a time I lay in my sleeping bag, counting ponies jumping gates. All that did was wake me up even more. My calculator was sitting next to the candlestick on the bedside table. I kept thinking what a wreck it was and that made me miserable.

To take my mind off it I watched the candleflame shadows for a bit. Mum had said blow out the candle before getting into bed. But it was cold out of bed and I knew I wasn't going to sleep yet. The shadows didn't move much because the flame burned steadily – we have double glazing. But when I turned on my side, the flame wobbled.

I was looking at the wall at the time and I saw this huge face. Pointed ears.

A sharp chin. A grinning mouth. There was a sort of flash too. As if moving car headlights had suddenly shone through the curtains then swept away. Only there isn't a road this side of our house. I tell you it didn't half make me jump. When I looked again, the face had gone.

The wind was getting worse. Whining through the trees and blowing so hard it even made the double glazing rattle. Poor old Oggie, I kept thinking.

He'll be soaked. Perhaps he was sitting on my windowsill this minute hoping I'd let him in?

I got out of bed and went to the window. I'd hardly got the curtains open, when a great racket of cats fighting nearly burst my eardrums. Two animal shadows were rolling about on the lawn outside. I felt for the windowcatch. Noticed over at the gravel pits some dots of light that shouldn't be there. Heard a cackle of laughter right next to my ear. All this happened at the same time.

My skin went all prickly and I shouted 'Oggie!' through the open window.

Something shot past my shoulder. *Going out.* A candleflame. That's what it looked like until it landed on the grass. Then from being yellow it turned a bright gingery red and grew taller and taller. Skinny arms and long twig fingers! Skinny legs too – birds' legs with claws instead of feet. On the very top was a big head with pointed wriggly ears, a sharp chin and grinning mouth. *And it had huge headlamp eyes.*

It was weird. Really scary! But I had to go on watching.

Suddenly it shrank to the size of a rose bush, but the eyes were still big. They beamed down on the cats. There was this terrible screech. One cat flew through the open window. The other just lay there quite still.

'Free, heeheehee . . .' I know that's what I heard. Same tinny voice.

I shut the window.

Outside the Thingy twirled round. Waved a long arm. 'Thanks Gill from Will . . .'

Well, I'm nearly sure that's what I heard.

The Thingy twirled again and went hopping and skipping over our fence. Across the building site. Leapt the far hedge, making for the gravel pits. Shrinking, shrinking until it was just another dot of light. Lost among the other dots on the marshy place.

Oggie had hidden under my bed and wouldn't come out. I saw his eyes glowing in the dark. Of course the candle had gone out. I was freezing, so I got into my sleeping bag. After a little while Oggie jumped up and curled against me. We got warm together and went to sleep.

'Gillie . . . Gillie . . .' Elise's voice.

'What?' I was so sleepy.

'I thought your cat was white.'

'He is.'

'Whose cat is that then? On your bed.'

That woke me. I sat up and looked at Oggie. It was Oggie. I'd know those eyes anywhere. One blue. One green. But his fur was bright ginger! I thought of telling her about Oggie's terrible fright, and all that I'd seen last night. But she never would have believed me.

'Look!' She was pointing at my calculator now. It sat where I'd put it last night, next to the candlestick. Not wrecked. Brand new!

'IMP DE LUXE,' I read. *De luxe? Imp* de luxe? For the first time I remembered an imp could be something else besides a calculator.

I looked it up in our dictionary before we had breakfast.

'A little devil,' it said. 'A wicked spirit.'

That didn't seem quite right. After all, my calculator had been fixed. And Oggie was okay even if he had turned ginger.

We started eating cornflakes.

'What a wild night,' Mum said. 'Did you see those imps on the marshy place by the gravel pits? Those lights.'

'They're called will o' the wisps,' Dad said.

'Marsh gas burning,' Les corrected him. He always thinks he knows everything. But now I understood and smiled to myself because I knew my

imp was where he wanted to be. *Home at last.*

Dad looked at Oggie sleeping, curled in his place by the chair leg. 'Where on earth did that cat come from?'

'Through my window,' I told him. 'Last night. I let him in. He's Oggie.'

'Don't talk daft,' Mum said. 'He's the wrong colour.'

'Whatever colour, he's a better hunter than Oggie. Have you seen that dead rat on our lawn this morning?' Dad spread out his hands. 'A monster!'

Oggie and I looked at each other. We weren't going to tell anyone what really happened. They would never believe us.